Hattie and the Wild Waves

A STORY FROM BROOKLYN
by BARBARA COONEY

SCHOLASTIC INC.
New York Toronto London Auckland Sydney

ISBN 0-590-45199-5

Copyright © 1990 by Barbara Cooney.
All rights reserved. Published by Scholastic Inc., 730 Broadway, New York, NY 10003, by arrangement with Viking Penguin, a division of Penguin Books USA Inc.

12 11 10 9 8 7 6 5 4 3 2 1   2 3 4 5 6 7/9

Printed in the U.S.A.   08

First Scholastic printing, March 1992

In memory of my mother,
Mae Bossert Cooney

and for her offspring

The big, red-brick house on Bushwick Avenue was the first house that Hattie could remember. Papa had built it for Mama right after they were married. Each room was finished and paneled in dark and gleaming woods, a different wood for each room: oak, mahogany, black walnut, butternut, and cherry. Papa was in the woodwork business, had been ever since he came to America and went to work with his brother Heinrich in Brooklyn. He wanted nothing but the best for Mama.

"When I grow up," said Pfiffi, as she looked at Mama's and Papa's wedding picture in the family album, "I shall be a beautiful bride, too." She tossed her curls.

"*Ja*," said Mama. "*Ja*." And she nodded.

"And I," said Vollie, who had been born the day the yacht *Volunteer* won the Cup Races, "I shall work with Papa in the business. And I shall make lots of money." He puffed up his chest with importance.

"And what about you, *mein Liebchen?*" Papa asked the child at his knee.

"I shall be a painter," said little Hattie promptly.

Pfiffi and Vollie exploded; they burst laughing. "*Dummkopf!*" they shrieked. "Little stupid head! Girls don't paint houses!"

But Hattie was not thinking about houses; she was thinking about the moon in the sky and the wind in the trees and the wild waves of the ocean.

The other people who lived in the house were Clara Gieseke, the cook; Little Mouse, Clara's small daughter; Mary Wagner, the maid; and a series of young girls who looked after the children. The nursemaids never stayed long. Pfiffi and Vollie teased them without mercy. Then Lena would scold sharply, maybe even slap a child. And that would be the end of Lena or Lizzie or Lili. Clara Gieseke and Mary Wagner, however, stayed on forever, gossiping in the kitchen, drinking coffee, and playing rummy with Pfiffi and Vollie. And Hattie, in the corner, contentedly scribbled away, making pictures on brown butcher's paper under the admiring eyes of Little Mouse.

"*Schön, schön,*" Little Mouse would murmur. "So pretty, pretty."

"*Fräulein* Hattie, always she is making such nice pictures," they said, looking up from their cards.

Hattie loved picture-making. Some of her happiest times were when she had a bad cold and Mama kept her in bed for two or three days running. Then she could make pictures from morning until night, interrupted only by bowls of milk toast and chicken broth.

On Sundays and holidays the uncles and aunts and
cousins gathered at the Bushwick Avenue house.
They arrived by carriage or horsecar, prosperous
and plump, Germans who had come to America in the
pursuit of happiness and fortune. They had founded
their lumber businesses and breweries across the river
from New York, in Brooklyn, in Flatbush and Greenpoint and Bushwick.

Around Mama's table they would sit, on high-
backed, heavy, nut-wood chairs, and eat. They ate
for hours: chicken and dumplings, great red roasts,
and pink hams swamped in raisin sauce.

"Ein klein bisschen Kartoffel?" Mama would ask. "A little
more potatoes?" For there was always a great deal of
Kartoffeln, clouds of mashed potatoes heaped high in
china dishes. And gravy boats full of dark delicious
gravy. And . . . and . . . and . . .

The children would grow restless; their eyes
drooped; and the parents went on with the family
gossip, sipping claret.

Finally Mama would rise and lead the company into the parlor, where she kept her two treasures, one a large oil painting hanging over the sofa, the other the beautiful rosewood piano that Papa had given her. The painting was *Cleopatra's Barge*, painted by Opa Krippendorf, who was Mama's father and an artist. It was his masterpiece.

"Beautiful," sighed the aunts.

And "Such a frame!" approved the uncles.

But Papa, who knew something about boats, pronounced the barge unseaworthy.

Later, Hattie went to her room and drew a beautiful barge.

"*Ja*," said Papa. "That one will float."

Sometimes Mama would sit down at her piano and play for the company. Her fingers would fly up and down the keyboard, while Hattie sat bewitched by the trills and grace notes of "The Spinning Song" and "Listen to the Mockingbird."

"Oh, to play like Mama," thought Hattie.

Mama's people were all musicians and artists. Mama had been a piano teacher. She was playing the organ in church when Papa first saw her. He married her three weeks later.

After the children were born, Mama would hold them on her lap and play lullabies. Soon she was giving them music lessons.

But "*Ach,*" said Mama, "Hattie's hands will never be large enough to stretch an octave. She will never get beyond 'The Happy Farmer.'"

"But I can whistle," said Hattie, "just like John the Coachman."

"*Ach,*" said Mama. "Nice girls don't whistle."

Mama taught the girls needlework, but Hattie's French knots were disgracefully grimy and her stitches were far from even.

"What beautiful needlework Pfiffi does!" the aunts exclaimed, unwrapping their Christmas handkerchiefs.

"*Ach*, but Hattie will never learn to sew," said Mama.

In fall and winter the children went to school. Then in the spring Mrs. Lehmann would come to stay at the Bushwick Avenue house and help Mama sew new clothes for summer. Those were trying days for Hattie, standing still while patterns were fitted and the pins pricked into her flesh. But Pfiffi enjoyed every minute, preening in front of the mirror as the pretty dresses took shape.

Every night Mama put Hattie's straight hair up in little leather-covered crimpers to make it curl.

"Trying to be pretty is a lot of work," sighed Hattie to Little Mouse.

But when Mama discovered Hattie sleeping with a clothespin on her nose to keep it from growing any longer, she scolded.

"*Ach*," said Mama, "just be glad you have all your limbs."

When the summer clothes were ready, the eyelet trim on the petticoats and nightgowns all threaded with pink and blue ribbons, Mama packed the trunks and the whole family moved out to Far Rockaway to the summer house beside the ocean. This was Hattie's favorite place.

There, too, the uncles and aunts and cousins came, taking the open horsecars to the Rockaways. On the shady verandas the parents rocked and drank lemonade and took deep breaths of the salt air. The women knitted and sewed and discussed the Family. The men discussed Business.

The city of New York was growing. People were crossing the East River and moving to the suburb of Brooklyn, to Flatbush and Greenpoint and Bushwick. Uncle Wilhelm expanded his brewery, and Uncle Otto opened an elegant beer garden. Papa built houses for the people, rows and rows of houses, all very much alike.

"But the people will get mixed up," said Hattie. "Especially in the fog."

"I will have to do something about that," said Papa.

And he painted the houses all different colors.

Sometimes Papa took the family sailing on his beautiful boat, the *Coronet*. The water sparkled. The waves slapped at the hull. At times Mama napped in her mahogany and pink velvet stateroom below. But always, Hattie stood in the bow. And the moist salt breezes took all the curl out of her hair.

When Hattie got home she ran up to her room and got out her paint box. Soon her walls were covered with pictures.

Oftentimes Hattie wandered down the beach by her-self, whistling and dreaming dreams while her little dog Ebbie scampered about her. The waves scalloped in and out, lapping at their feet. The sky was the blue of heaven, and the sea went on forever.

"I wish that summer would never end," thought Hattie.

Sometimes the ocean turned green and wild, and the sky grew black.

"Oh, Ebbie," she would say, picking up the little dog, "what are the wild waves saying?"

Whatever they were saying, they had the answer. That she knew as she walked beside the sea.

So the summers passed at Far Rockaway. Fall came and they returned to Bushwick Avenue. The leaves fell, and Pfiffi and Vollie and Hattie went back to school.

One winter day, as the children bent over their homework, Papa brought them a remarkable piece of news. He had just bought the family a new summer house called "The Oaks," a house as big as a castle, far out on Long Island, far, far away from Far Rockaway.

"But, *lieber* Max," said Mama, "I wouldn't know how to run such a house."

"You will, *mein Schatzi*," said Papa. "For you will have a butler and footmen and upstairs maids and downstairs maids and, of course, Clara Gieseke in the kitchen and John the Coachman in the stables."

"We will be like princesses!" cried Pfiffi.

"And a prince," said Vollie, not wanting to be left out.

Only Hattie was unsure. What would the wild waves be saying at Far Rockaway next summer? She would not find out, for Papa sold the Far Rockaway house, and they moved far out on Long Island to the big new house.

Every morning the children's horses were brought around to the porte-cochère for their daily rides.

And every morning Mama put on little rubber boots and a black sateen apron and went into her conservatory to water the plants.

In the afternoon there were tennis parties. Papa had given Hattie a tame macaw, which was trained to retrieve tennis balls. Oh, that was another wonder of this new life!

Some days Little Mouse and Hattie walked in the deer park, their arms around each other, telling their secrets, as girls do.

"I am going to be a teacher," said Little Mouse.

"And I," said Hattie, "am going to be an artist."

"I know," said Little Mouse.

Now and then the uncles and aunts and cousins came out on the Long Island Railroad for visits, and everyone was much impressed with "The Oaks." But it wasn't the same as Far Rockaway.

Suitors began to come courting Pfiffi. Clara Gieseke had no time now for gossip and rummy, no time for *Fräulein* Hattie. Little Mouse was busy all the time cutting up vegetables and polishing silver. And John the Coachman was always having to meet guests at the station. For there were many parties nowadays.

So Hattie walked in the deer park by herself, with Ebbie. Or she took her paint box down to the pond and painted the black swans from China.

One day a new suitor appeared. He was in the lumber business. He had a white bull terrier named Snide and an automobile. He was very suitable. And he was the one Pfiffi chose.

Then Mrs. Lehmann and an old woman known simply as "Tante from Jersey" took over one of the upstairs sitting rooms and proceeded to make Pfiffi's trousseau, hemstitching and cross-stitching and featherstitching. They stayed for weeks. Mama herself did all the monograms. But the wedding dress itself came from Paris.

"*Fräulein* Hattie will be next," said Mrs. Lehmann. She smiled a big smile full of gold teeth.

The aunts all took their furs out of the camphor closet. Everyone put on their finest clothes and came to the wedding. There was caviar and sweetbreads in Madeira wine; there were jumbo squabs and artichokes with hollandaise sauce; there was tutti-frutti ice cream and champagne and Corona cigars. Hattie was the maid of honor; Vollie was the best man; Papa gave Pfiffi away; Mama cried; and Pfiffi was a beautiful bride.

"I am not *Fraulein* Pfiffi anymore," said the bride proudly. "From now on I am Mrs. Joseph Patrick Counihan."

"I like being a *Fraulein*," said Hattie to Little Mouse. "A Mrs. is forever, Mouse."

"Someday maybe we will want it to be forever," said Little Mouse.

Now Vollie became a businessman. All summer he rode the Long Island Railroad with Papa, back and forth to work in town.

"If only there were a nice hotel in Brooklyn," Papa wished.

And since there wasn't, he built one.

When it was finished, Papa sold the Bushwick Avenue house.

In the wintertime, Mama and Papa and Hattie went to live on the top floor of Papa's hotel, with a splendid view of the East River and New York City. But Vollie preferred to live at his club.

At mealtimes Gus the Waiter trundled in a little cart bearing silver-domed dishes out of which came their breakfasts, lunches, and dinners.

From the parlor where Mama had her rosewood piano and *Cleopatra's Barge* Hattie sketched tugs and cargo boats going up and down the river. Looking downriver from Papa's library, she could paint the Statue of Liberty and the ocean beyond. But too often Hattie had to go shopping or play Russian bank with Mama.

Downstairs, on Sundays, Hattie sat by herself in the hotel's Palm Room under the beautiful blue and white and gold ceiling and listened to a string orchestra play tunes from *Die Fledermaus* and *The Merry Widow*. If only Little Mouse could see this room and hear the music, thought Hattie. But Little Mouse had gone away to become a teacher.

On Tuesdays Hattie went with Mama and Papa to the opera at the Academy of Music. Then Mama wore her diamond tiara and draped her powdered shoulders in tulle. They would sit in their seats in Box Four above the kettledrum. From time to time Mama would hand around the little silver box of candy jujubes. Papa, taking one, would smile proudly.

One Tuesday evening, as waves of music filled the opera house, a young woman, down on the stage, sang her heart out. Hattie, in Box Four, sat transfixed.

The time had come, she realized, for her to paint her heart out.

The next day Hattie put on her coat and hat and marched down to the Art Institute. Her business accomplished, she took the trolley out to Coney Island. It was cold and blowy and spitting snow. Most of the rides were shut down, but the little booth containing the wax gypsy fortune-teller was open. Hattie approached the glass-fronted booth. She slipped a coin in the slot.

"What is my future to be?" she whispered.

A little pink card appeared in the opening below.

"You will make beautiful pictures," said the card.

Hattie walked along the deserted beach holding the little card. The waves reared up; they crested and broke.

"You will make beautiful, beautiful pictures," said the wild waves. Over and over they said the words.

"Oh, yes," breathed Hattie. "Oh, yes, I shall."

"I have something to tell you," Hattie said to Mama and Papa the next morning at breakfast.

"*Was ist los?*" asked Mama anxiously. "Is something the matter?"

Hattie folded her napkin. She put it in her napkin ring. Her eyes shone.

"I am going to be an artist," she said.

"Just like Opa," said Mama, smiling.

"No," said Hattie. "Just like me."

For all their help I thank Alice Cooney Frelinghuysen, Metropolitan Museum of Art;
Claire Lamers, Brooklyn Historical Society;
and José Gonzales, Bushwick United Head Start.